FiZZ and the POLICE DOG TRYOUTS

BOOK 1

For Rodney, Austin and Georgia. L.G.

For Millie. S.M.K.

First published by Allen & Unwin in 2016

Allen & Unwin
83 Alexander Street
Crows Nest NSW 2065
Australia
Phone: (61 2) 8425 0100
Email: info@allenandunwin.com
Web: www.allenandunwin.com

A Cataloguing-in-Publication entry is available
from the National Library of Australia
www.trove.nla.gov.au

ISBN 978 1 76011 285 1

Cover and text design by Stephen Michael King and Trish Hayes
Set in 15pt Berkeley Oldstyle Book by Trish Hayes, Stingart
Printed in Australia by Griffin Press

10 9 8 7 6 5

The paper in this book is FSC® certified.
FSC® promotes environmentally responsible,
socially beneficial and economically viable
management of the world's forests.

www.lesleygibbes.com
www.stephenmichaelking.com

FiZZ

and the
POLICE DOG
TRYOUTS

LESLEY GIBBES

ILLUSTRATED BY
STEPHEN MICHAEL KING

ALLEN&UNWIN
SYDNEY · MELBOURNE · AUCKLAND · LONDON

Benny

Puff-Pup   Fluff-Pup

Sergeant Stern

Fizz's mother

Bruno

Bella

Crystal

Razor

Fizz's
father

Fizz

Tom Whittaker

Amadeus

CONTENTS

With special thanks to Margaret Connolly, Sue Flockhart, Erica Wagner, Stephen Michael King and Trish Hayes.

L.G.

Chapter 1

I Want to be a Police Dog

'I'm not a little puppy anymore!'
sang Fizz to the world.
'I'm all grown up and
ready to find a job.'

Fizz knew exactly what
job he wanted.

'I want to be a police
dog,' he said, puffing out
his chest.

It would be the
perfect job for Fizz.
Police dogs were brave:
Fizz was brave.

Police dogs were clever:
Fizz was clever.

Police dogs were fast:
Fizz was super-fast.
He was the fastest
dog at Sunnyvale
Boarding House.

But there was one tiny problem. Police dogs look like this:

and Fizz looks like this: a small cute ball of white, fizzy, fuzzy fur.

How unfair to feel so brave and bold on the inside, but to look so cute and cuddly on the outside!

The day Fizz told his family he wanted to be a police dog they tried to talk him out of it.

'No one in our family has ever been a police dog, son. We're Bologneses; we're show dogs and companion dogs, not working dogs,' said Fizz's father. 'Wouldn't you rather be a champion show dog like me?'

His mother didn't understand either. 'You could get hurt and your pretty fur would get all dirty, sugarplum. Why don't you be a little lap dog like your sister Bella? Then you'll stay safe and clean.'

'But Mum, I don't want to be a lap dog,' said Fizz, his fluffy tail drooping.

'Or,' continued his mother, 'you could be the handbag dog for a famous actress, like your sister Crystal. She's travelled the world three times over.

'And your brothers Puff-Pup and Fluff-Pup just love being companion dogs for old Mrs Winterbottom. Plenty of cuddles and treats, you know.'

'But Mum, you're not listening. I don't want to be any of those things,' said Fizz. 'I want adventure! I want to run and chase and bark. I want to bail-up burglars, catch crooks and save the day. What I really, really want is to be a police dog. I'm sure I'd make a good one. Remember the time I sniffed out the missing chew treats for Mrs Winterbottom?'

His parents frowned. 'Son, you just don't look like a police dog,' said his father firmly. 'Mum and I don't want you to get your hopes up in case you're disappointed, that's all. And besides, Ms Trunchon from the Dog Employment Department will help you find a suitable job when you have your interview tomorrow. She'll find the perfect job for a dog like you.'

Fizz trudged out of the boarding house and into the exercise yard.

'I don't want to be a companion dog or a show dog, and I don't want to see Ms Trunchon,' said Fizz, looking out beyond the boarding house gates towards the city. 'I want to be a police dog.'

Chapter 2

The Advertisement

'What's wrong, Fizz?' asked Tom Whittaker. He put down his newspaper and took a bite out of his bacon roll.

Tom was the grounds-keeper at Sunnyvale Boarding House for Dogs, and he had known Fizz since he was a pup.

Fizz loved helping Tom whenever there was digging to be done in the gardens or an adventure to be had. Once they had rescued puppies that were lost in the huge grounds around the old boarding house.

'I want to be a police dog. I don't look like a police dog, and Dad wants me to be like him, and Mum wants me to be like my brothers and sisters. But I'm *not* like them. I don't want to be pampered and preened. I'm rough and tough,' Fizz blurted out. He slumped down next to Tom under the shade of the old jacaranda tree.

Tom gave Fizz a firm, understanding pat.

'You know, Fizz, it's not the size of the dog in the fight, but the size of the fight in the dog that counts.' He took another bite of his bacon roll.

'What do you mean?' asked Fizz.

'It's not what you look like that counts, Fizz, it's what you can do. Do you think you can do everything a police dog can do?'

'You bet I can! If only I had the chance to prove myself,' said Fizz, sitting up straight.

'Well then, you'll want to hear this,' said Tom, reading out an advertisement from his newspaper.

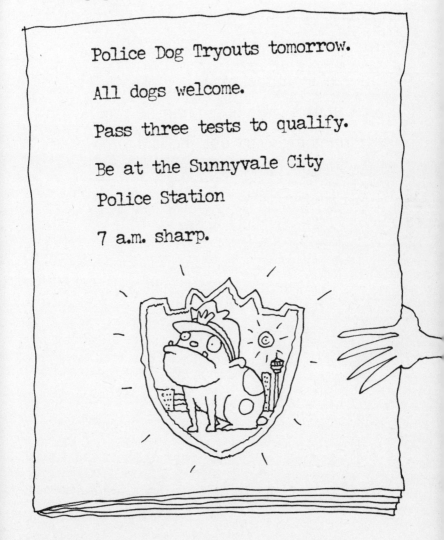

Police Dog Tryouts tomorrow.

All dogs welcome.

Pass three tests to qualify.

Be at the Sunnyvale City Police Station

7 a.m. sharp.

'If this is your dream, Fizz, then you should go for it,' said Tom. 'You don't know what you can do until you try.'

Fizz thought about Ms Trunchon and the dog employment interview. Then he thought about the police dog tryouts. His skin tingled with goosebumps.

'I'm going to try out!' he said.

Chapter 3

The Tryouts

izz woke early with butterflies in his stomach. The police dog tryouts were today at 7 a.m., and he didn't want to be late. He tried to eat his breakfast, tiptoed past his parents' room, and sprinted

across the exercise yard and out of the boarding house gates. His head was spinning and his heart was thumping.

This was the day he'd been waiting for.

'Today I'm going to become a police dog!' barked Fizz. 'I just know it!'

Fizz turned onto the main road and headed straight for the city. It was a hot and dusty walk but his feet hardly touched the ground. All he could think of was how good it was going to feel to become a police dog.

At last Fizz arrived at busy Sunnyvale City. The morning sun was already lighting up the tall city buildings. Fizz ran down the street, dodging in and out of people's legs. He could see the dark brick walls and clear glossy windows of the Sunnyvale City Police Station at the end of Main Street.

But as Fizz got closer, his stomach squirmed. Something wasn't right. He stopped and blinked. He couldn't believe his eyes. The wide pavement outside the police station was bustling with the largest pack of dogs Fizz had ever seen. A spectacular mix of Boxers, German Shepherds, Dobermans, Dalmatians, Wolfhounds and Rottweilers – all big and barking – jostled for a place at the front of the line.

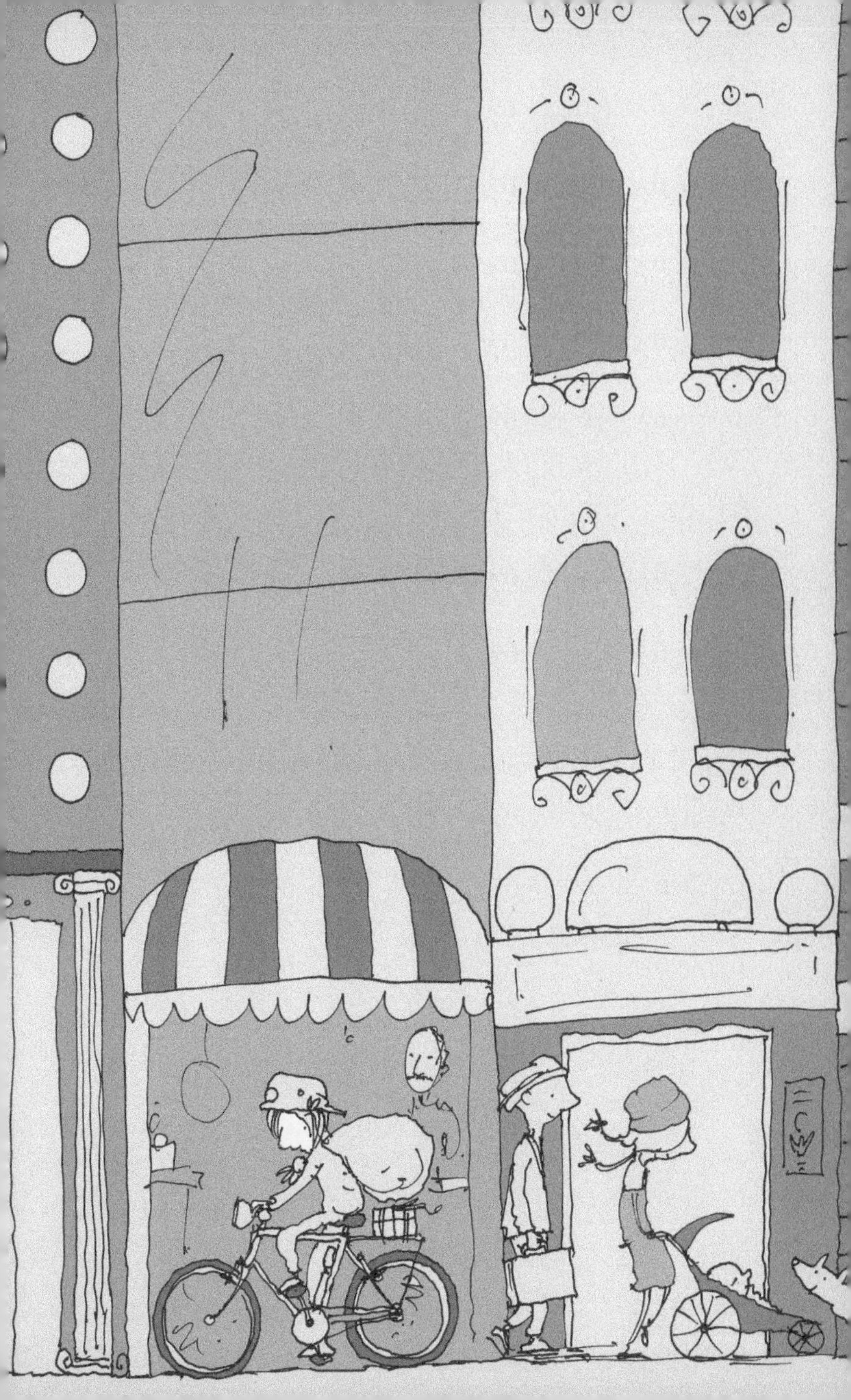

Fizz hadn't thought that lots of other dogs would want to try out too. His fluffy ears sagged.

He walked past every dog until he found the very end of the line, far beyond the door of the police station. He waited.

'Hi, I'm Benny,' said a chocolate-brown Labrador in front of him.

'I'm Fizz,' said Fizz, glancing up at all the other dogs. He was the smallest, whitest, fluffiest dog in the queue.

'I know. It's crazy, right? There must be a hundred dogs here today. What do you think the three tests will be?' asked Benny.

'I don't know,' said Fizz. He'd been so excited he hadn't given it much thought until now.

'My dad said last year the competitors had to jump over a four-metre brick wall and land with all four paws on a spot the size of a dog bowl. Dad made me practise every day for a month. What skills have you been practising?'

Fizz's throat tightened. The other dogs had been training for months and he hadn't practised a thing.

'I didn't know about the tryouts until yesterday,' said Fizz, shaking the fur from over his eyes.

'Dad wants me to be a police dog, but I reckon being a rescue dog would be fun too. What do you think?' asked Benny, wagging his tail like a windscreen wiper.

Fizz didn't get a chance to answer. Two large dogs had arrived and were bulldozing their way through the crowd.

'Make way for the winner!' they shouted.

Chapter 4

Here Comes Amadeus

'Out of the way, losers! Here comes Amadeus!' barked a large, dopey Boxer named Bruno.

'Amadeus is the next City Police Dog. None of you stand a chance!' growled a nasty red Ridgeback named Razor. He pushed his way ahead of Benny and Fizz.

'Go on, go home, you wimps,' said Bruno with a silly grin on his face. 'Amadeus is here.'

'Who's Amadeus?' whispered Fizz into Benny's ear.

'No one nice. Stay out of his way,' said Benny, pushing Fizz back into the crowd.

Fizz and Benny saw a long shadow creep in front of them. Benny's jaw dropped. A group of Dalmatians whimpered. Fizz's fur spiked like a porcupine. Amadeus had arrived!

His neck was thick and strong, and his massive chest was set between two muscular sloping shoulders. His dense fur was as black as midnight, and his eyes were cold and cruel.

Amadeus stood tall and glared at the long line of dogs, just waiting for someone to catch his eye. He saw Fizz.

'Well, well, look what we have here, boys,' said Amadeus, pushing his nose into Fizz's fluffy face. 'A giant cotton ball!'

Bruno and Razor roared with laughter.

Fizz was tiny beside Amadeus and only a fraction of his weight.

'Get a load of this fur. What's your name? Sweetheart? Cutie? Poppet?' jeered Amadeus.

'It's Fizz.' Fizz shook down his fur and stretched up as tall as he could.

Amadeus looked at him as if he were a piece of fluff stuck on his paw. 'Your name's Fizz? Even better! Well, Fizzy, the Miss Fluffy Puppy tryouts are next door. This line is for the big boys.' Amadeus looked at Bruno and Razor and sneered.

'Yeah, Powder Puff, this line's for the big boys,' said Bruno.

Razor circled Fizz, flashing his yellow teeth. His breath was stale and hot. He and Bruno had been in Amadeus's gang since they were puppies. 'Off you go then!' he teased.

Fizz didn't move. 'I'm here to try out, and I'm going to try out.'

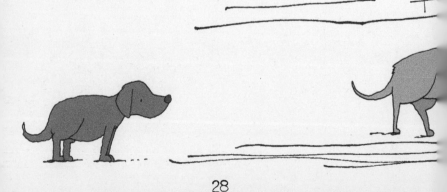

Razor and Bruno were stunned. No one spoke to Amadeus like that.

'What!' snarled Amadeus, snapping his jaws like a pair of garden shears. 'You want to be a police dog? You've got to be joking. You look more like a fluffy slipper! You're out of your league here, Powder Puff. Time for you to go home!'

Amadeus flexed his enormous muscles and flicked his back paws, shooting gravel at Fizz and all the dogs near him in the line. 'I'm the next City Police Dog. Not you. Not any of you. Get it?' And with that he pushed his way to the front, with Bruno and Razor in tow.

Fizz watched until Amadeus was out of sight, then his tail drooped and his chest deflated like a day-old birthday balloon. The tryouts weren't going to be easy. The other dogs were rough and fierce, and Amadeus was the biggest, nastiest dog Fizz had ever met. And worst of all, he had taken an instant dislike to Fizz!

Attention! Attention, please!' called a police officer in a smart blue uniform. 'My name is Sergeant Stern and I'll be running the Sunnyvale City Police Dog Tryouts today. Competing dogs, please follow me into the back compound. No parents, thank you.'

Fizz and Benny followed the pack of dogs into an exercise yard behind the police station. It was a big space, with old boxes and a getaway car from a foiled bank robbery. Sergeant Stern waited for the competing dogs to assemble. Finally, all the dogs were ready. Fizz and Benny listened as Sergeant Stern spoke.

'To be a police dog you must pass all three tests,' announced Sergeant Stern. 'The Bark Test, the Scare Test and the Chase-and-Catch Test. Fail any test and you're out!'

A nervous whisper broke out amongst the crowd of competing dogs. Amadeus pushed his way in beside Fizz.

'You'll never make it past the first test, Fairy Floss,' hissed Amadeus.

Fizz pretended not to hear. He didn't want Amadeus to think he was scared.

'Settle down, everyone,' continued Sergeant Stern. 'I'm looking for one police dog and one police dog only. We will begin with the Bark Test.'

Sergeant Stern ordered the dogs into ten long lines.

'If your bark is loud enough, you'll pass. If it's not, you're out!' said Sergeant Stern, pointing to the exit sign. Fizz loved barking but he wasn't sure his bark would be loud enough.

'May the best dog win,' said Sergeant Stern, clapping his hands as he walked over to the first line of dogs.

'That'll be me!' boasted Amadeus loudly to the crowd. 'Watch and learn, Powder Puff. This is how the big dogs do it!'

Amadeus took in a deep breath. His chest expanded. He gave the deepest, loudest bark Fizz had ever heard. The other dogs joined in and the air filled with a roaring noise that bounced and echoed around the yard. Sergeant Stern walked the lines listening to each dog in turn.

'Pass. Pass. Too soft, you're out. Out. Out. Out. Pass. Out. Out. Out. You'll have to be louder than that, son, out!' Sergeant Stern stood in front of Amadeus. Amadeus boomed a deafening bark.

'Impressive, Amadeus. You've got your father's voice.'

Amadeus smirked. He came from a long line of police dogs and his father had been coaching him for the tryouts since he was a pup.

Fizz was next. His nose was dry and his legs felt like jelly. He drew in a deep breath.

Amadeus grinned. 'Look everyone, Powder Puff's about to squeal like a squeaky toy.' Then he stomped his back foot down hard onto Fizz's paw.

Fizz felt a burning pain and cried out, 'Eeeeeeeeeooooooooooooooooooowwwwww weeeeeeeeeeeeeeeeccccccchhhhhhh!'

Eeeeeeee

The high-pitched screech cut through the deepest barks of the largest dogs. It seared through ears and sent dogs howling in pain. Even Bruno whined. Sergeant Stern stood still in front of Fizz. Fizz closed his eyes tight.

'Excellent, Fizz!' he said. 'You could stop traffic with a bark like that. Pass!'

Fizz caught his breath. His paw throbbed but he no longer felt the pain. He had passed the Bark Test.

'That was awesome, Fizz,' said Benny.

'You won't be so lucky next time,' sneered Amadeus. He swatted Fizz with his black bristly tail. 'I'm watching you!'

Chapter 6

The Scare Test

More than half the dogs had failed the Bark Test, but Fizz, Benny, Bruno, Razor and Amadeus had all passed. The Scare Test was next.

'I've been practising my scary face every day. Want to see?' asked Benny. He pulled a hideous face.

'Wow, that's ugly,' laughed Fizz. 'You look like a rotten cabbage. You'll pass the Scare Test for sure.'

'Show me your scary face,'
said Benny. Fizz stuck out his
tongue and went cross-eyed.
Razor and Bruno sneaked up
to watch.

'Is that the best you can do?' said Razor,
pretending to tremble. Bruno laughed so
hard he forgot to look where he was going
and stumbled into Amadeus.

'Watch it, dopey!' snapped Amadeus.
He glared at Fizz. 'You passed the Bark Test,
Powder Puff, but no one's going to be scared
of a piece of fluff like you!'

'Don't listen to him,' said Benny.

But Fizz began to worry. Maybe Amadeus was right. No one was going to be frightened of a little, white, fluffy dog.

'Right everyone, it's time to show me what you've got,' called Sergeant Stern.

Fizz's muscles tightened and his sore paw throbbed. He knew he had to do something big, something different, something surprising. But what?

'Start when you're ready,' called Sergeant Stern, casting his eye over the crowd of dogs.

Fizz was thinking…so hard his head ached. If he wasn't scary, he'd be out! If he failed the test, he'd have to see Ms Trunchon for a dog employment interview. Then he had an idea. He crawled through the legs of the growling, snarling dogs and stood at the front of the pack, face to face with Amadeus.

Amadeus bared his long fangs and his eyes glowed red and fierce.

Fizz could feel them burning deep into his eyes. He stared back bravely. And then it happened. With a flash of white, Fizz's long fluffy hair shot up into wild hackles, like a razor-sharp mohawk. His brilliant white teeth flashed. His tail cut through the air like a knife. Fizz was unexpectedly scary.

Razor whimpered. Bruno covered his eyes. Several Dalmatians hid behind Sergeant Stern's legs. Benny went cold. Even Amadeus was speechless.

'That's a pass, Fizz,' called Sergeant Stern.

Chapter 7

The Final Test

'Whoa, Fizz,' said Benny. 'You're amazing! You should've seen Amadeus after the Scare Test. He was so mad I thought he was going to explode.'

'You looked scary, too. I bet Bruno has nightmares about cabbages now,' laughed Fizz.

'Would the ten remaining dogs please take their places for the Chase-and-Catch Test,' called Sergeant Stern.

Fizz, Benny, Razor, Bruno and Amadeus were all still in the competition, along with five other dogs.

'Congratulations. You are the top ten dogs today, but only one of you will become the next Sunnyvale City Police Dog. This final test will decide the winner. Please form one line for the Chase-and-Catch,' said Sergeant Stern.

A police officer disguised as a burglar joined Sergeant Stern. The 'burglar' was dressed in black, with an eye-mask and a big black hat.

'Catch the burglar and bring him down for a speedy arrest,' instructed Sergeant Stern. 'You have five minutes and five minutes only to bring the burglar to the ground. Take too long and you're out!'

Fizz felt confident about the chase because he was a fast runner. But he wasn't a big dog, and he didn't have the weight that was needed to pull a man to the ground. Fizz looked at the burglar. He was nimble, and fast on his feet. If Fizz wanted to be a police dog, he would have to pass this final test. But how ever was he going to do it?

Fizz watched as dog after dog tried to bring the burglar down. Razor, Bruno and Benny had all tried, but the burglar was still standing.

'Bad luck, Benny. You almost had him,' said Fizz.

'I don't mind,' said Benny, looking at his feet. 'I really want to be a rescue dog anyway.'

Only Fizz and Amadeus were left.
And Fizz was next. If he couldn't bring the
burglar to his knees, his dream of being a
police dog was over. He'd spend the rest of
his life as a show dog. Fizz's nose went dry
and his heart raced.

'This is it, Fizz! It's between you and
Amadeus now. Good luck! You can do it,
I know you can,' said Benny.

51

Click

'Ready, Fizz?' asked
Sergeant Stern. Fizz took
a long, deep breath, then
nodded. 'Remember, Fizz, you have only five
minutes,' warned Sergeant Stern. 'Take your
place at the starting line. Ready. Set. Go!' He
pressed the start button on his stopwatch.

The burglar made a speedy escape. Fizz
raced after him. His white paws thumped
and skidded on the loose dirt of the
compound. Fizz pushed his legs harder and
faster. He chased the burglar in and out of
old crates and boxes.

'Four minutes left,' called Sergeant Stern.

Fizz was right behind the burglar.

'Jump, Fizz, jump!' yelled Benny.

Fizz pushed on with all his strength. His muscles burned. Suddenly, a sharp pain shot through his sore paw. As Fizz stumbled, the burglar sped away.

'Keep trying!' yelled Benny.

Fizz ran faster and faster. He closed in on the burglar.

'Three minutes left,' called Sergeant Stern.

'Jump!' howled Benny.

But Fizz didn't jump. He kept on running…right past the burglar.

'What are you doing, Fizz? Go back!' yelled Benny.

'Loser!' said Amadeus. 'You're supposed to catch him, not race him, Powder Puff!'

Fizz searched frantically for a way to get up higher. If his paw was too sore to jump the burglar in one big leap, then he'd have do it in smaller ones.

He saw his chance. He ran towards the abandoned getaway car and jumped onto the rusty bonnet. His claws screeched as he slid towards the windscreen…*thud*. Fizz scrambled onto the roof of the car and waited.

'He's got a plan!' shouted Benny. 'Watch, everyone!'

'Two minutes left,' called Sergeant Stern.

Fizz leapt high into the air just as the burglar was passing the car. With his fur flying in all directions, Fizz landed – *thump* – right on the burglar's head. The burglar stumbled, but Fizz held on tight. Then he pushed the burglar's black hat down hard over his eyes.

'The burglar can't see!' yelled a large Dalmatian to the crowd.

The man wriggled the
hat but it was stuck fast
over his eyes.

'One minute left,' called Sergeant
Stern, holding his stopwatch aloft.

Quick as a flea, Fizz grabbed the burglar's
trousers and tugged them to the ground. Then
he clamped the burglar's black belt with his
teeth and pulled it tight around the man's
ankles. Fizz pulled and pulled till his jaw
ached. With both feet tied together and the
hat over his eyes, the burglar started to lose
his balance. Fizz yanked harder. The burglar
wobbled and tottered.

I'm going to win, thought Fizz. Just one more pull and I'll bring him down.

'He's going to do it! He's going to win!' shouted Benny, bouncing like a beach ball.

Fizz was dizzy with anticipation. *I'm going to be a police dog. I really am!*

Then out of nowhere, a dark and menacing body leapt over Fizz's head and landed heavily upon the burglar's chest. The crowd gasped.

The burglar toppled to the ground. Sergeant Stern pressed the stop button on his stopwatch.

'Your time's up, Powder Puff!' growled Amadeus.

Fizz crumpled with disappointment. Amadeus had brought the burglar down. His dream of being a police dog was over. Amadeus would be the new Sunnyvale City Police Dog. Bruno and Razor howled with delight.

I'll never be anything more than a lap dog,
thought Fizz as he trudged back to where
Benny and Sergeant Stern were waiting.

'I'm so sorry, Fizz,' said Benny, running
to meet him.

'The winner,' announced Sergeant Stern,
'of the City Police Dog tryouts, and our
brand new Sunnyvale City Police Dog is…
Amadeus.'

Amadeus gave out a loud victory howl. Razor and Bruno barked madly.

'Congratulations, Amadeus,' said Fizz politely.

'The best dog won, Powder Puff,' growled Amadeus. 'I'm the new City Police Dog. Don't you forget it! It's time for you to go back to puppy school where you belong.' Then he turned his back on Fizz and howled at the crowd, 'I am Amadeus the Awesome!'

Chapter 8

I Must Be Dreaming

'I'm sorry, Fizz,' said Sergeant Stern patting Fizz on the back. 'You did very well but you just don't look like a police dog.'

Fizz drooped. Even Sergeant Stern thought he was just a little fluffy dog.

'Which is a very good thing,' continued Sergeant Stern, 'because it makes you perfect for our Undercover Dog Division. All that fuzzy fur is the perfect disguise for a keen-eyed undercover police dog like you.'

Fizz tingled all over. Surely he was dreaming! Benny was bouncing and everyone was cheering – except Amadeus, who muttered something nasty under his breath.

'Congratulations, Undercover Agent Fizz,' said Sergeant Stern. 'I know you're going to do a great job!'

Fizz puffed out his fluffy chest so far he thought he would burst. If only his family was here to share in his excitement.

Then, from way back in the crowd came a bustling and a rustling and his family burst through the cheering dogs.

'The first undercover police dog in our family! I just couldn't be prouder,' said Fizz's father.

'You'll look after all that beautiful fur won't you, sugarplum. After all, it's an

important part of your undercover disguise,'
said Fizz's mother.

'Yes, Mum, I promise,' said Fizz. Bella,
Crystal, Puff-Pup and Fluff-Pup gave Fizz
a happy group hug.

'How did you know I was here?' asked
Fizz.

'Tom told us,' said Fizz's mother. 'He
knows we only want the best for you. And
besides, he knew you could do it.'

Fizz snuggled into his mother's soft fur.

'What's all this!' said Sergeant Stern, breaking up the family gathering. 'It's straight home and into bed for you, Fizz. Training starts tomorrow!'

'Whoo-hoo!' cheered Fizz. 'I can't wait!'

From the Author and the Illustrator

When Lesley Gibbes discovered that her father-in-law's childhood nickname was 'Fizz', she knew it was the perfect name for her fluffy undercover police dog. But it was her two naughty Jack Russell terriers, Porsche and Cosworth, who were the real inspiration for Fizz. Just like Fizz, they're clever, brave and fast. And even though they are only the size of a tomcat, they both think they're as big and as bold as a German Shepherd.

When Stephen Michael King was a boy he liked to draw dogs: dogs scuba diving, driving cars, playing guitar or flying into outerspace… anything he could imagine a normal dog doing on any normal day. Now Stephen is married with two grown children, one parrot and three dogs, and he still finds himself drawing dogs: dogs in cars, on motorbikes, dressed in silly costumes and chasing robbers.

Their picture book *Scary Night*, written by Lesley Gibbes and illustrated by Stephen Michael King, was named an Honour Book in the 2015 CBCA Book of the Year Awards for Early Childhood.

The story continues in **Book 2**

FIZZ and the DOG ACADEMY RESCUE